V   ~.von

J. M. Vignes-Dumas

Pen Press

First published in Great Britain by Pen Press

All paper used in the printing of this book has been made from wood grown in managed, sustainable forests.

ISBN 978-1-78003-440-9

Printed and bound in the UK
Pen Press is an imprint of
Indepenpress Publishing Limited
25 Eastern Place
Brighton
BN2 1GJ

A catalogue record of this book is available from
the British Library

Cover design by Jacqueline Abromeit

The stories about the Indian Ocean islands Seychelles, Mauritius, Rodriguez and La Reunion are in honour of my late husband, John Lewis Winsley Dumas, (both of us are Mauritian) who died in June 2009 in Malvern Victoria, in our home.

In June 2009 as a newly qualified freelance journalist (Cengage Education, N.S.W.) I was on a working holiday (alone) involved in a project concerning the second last Shah of Iran, Shah Ahmed Shah Pahlavi who was in exile in Mauritius in 1941.

Contents

Sister Mary and the Tasmanian Devil Ghost

Tasmania is the only island state of Australia and Hobart is the capital.

In Hobart on New Year's Day 2004 it was a very warm morning. Sister Mary went to St Peter's Catholic Church to clean it at approximately 5.30 am before huge crowds of people came to church to celebrate New Year's Day. As she approached the church, Sister Mary could see through the front door window a very bright light behind the altar. She thought that it was 86-year-old Father McGee behind the altar with his torch looking for something inside the very dark wooden altar cupboard.

As Sister Mary opened the front door she said in a very loud cheerful voice, "Happy New Year, Father McGee, I shall go to your office to fetch the vacuum cleaner."

"Take your time my dear," said a voice, but the voice was not that of Father McGee. Puzzled, Sister Mary thought perhaps it was the new cleaner speaking to her. After all, Father McGee was 86 years old and was finding it hard to get out of bed at such an early hour and had been considering a new cleaner for several months.

"Where are you?" said Sister Mary.

"I am inside the cupboard behind the altar," said the voice. "For I am a Tasmanian Devil Ghost."

"Stop joking," laughed Sister Mary.

"No, true," said the Tasmanian Devil Ghost.

A Tasmanian Devil is a large hairy animal that looks like a large rat.

Sister Mary really started to get scared and chanted "Hail Mary full of grace" to calm her nerves for she really thought that she was speaking to THE DEVIL. "Well," said Sister Mary in a rather embarrassed voice, "I confess to stealing a bottle of whisky that belonged to Father McGee. I am truly sorry, my goodness, all night I had a bellyache and a dizzy head, never, never again.

"Now then," said Sister Mary, "I have no time to waste, get out of your hiding place immediately."

"As I said, I am stuck inside the cupboard," said the Tasmanian Devil Ghost. "My master, Captain Phillip McWilliams, said that I am a genius."

"A genius?" said Sister Mary. Laughing, she was thankful that she was not speaking to THE DEVIL.

"By the way my name is Gerry, and your name is?"

The nun replied with pride, "Sister Mary Joseph."

Gerry told Sister Mary that he could speak several languages because Captain Phillip and he used to travel to many countries, but mainly stayed in Papua, New Guinea due to the fine weather.

This is Gerry's story, how he became a Tasmanian Devil Ghost.:

Papua, New Guinea November 2003

Most evenings Captain McWilliams and I would watch the sunset. While watching the sunset the Captain would play his bagpipes. The Captain loved to travel but he still felt homesick for Scotland. Captain McWilliams and Father McGee had been friends since their university days in Scotland.

In late November 2003 Captain McWilliams and Gerry were preparing a crate full of Scotch whisky for Father McGee as a Christmas present. Gerry stood inside the crate placing each bottle carefully so that they would not break. That day the Captain had had too much to drink and accidentally nailed down the crate cover forgetting that Gerry was still inside the crate. He then went outside to watch the sunset and play his bagpipes.

Gerry shouted and shouted to be let out of the crate, but the Captain could not hear him due to the bagpipe music. This is how Gerry became a Tasmanian Devil Ghost.

When Father McGee received the small crate from Papua, New Guinea, he placed the crate inside the altar cupboard behind the altar. This is why Gerry was inside the altar cupboard.

Gerry's ghost is still inside the cupboard behind St Peter's altar.

The Special Interview

One very cold afternoon a little old man sat in a badly lit Melbourne café. The old man was Mr Abraham Heaven, a retired school teacher so he liked to tell people. On that day he wore a huge woollen coat. On the front of the coat was embroidered in large capital letters the word BELIEVE and on the back of the coat was embroidered also in large capital letters the word TRUST.

An hour or two had passed and suddenly a schoolboy named Peter entered the café to buy a packet of chips. As he paid the assistant for the packet of chips, he noticed Mr Abraham Heaven and asked him if he knew where Spirit Room Hotel was located. Mr Heaven replied, "Child, you know the answer to your question, you just want to know whether an old man can still think clearly."

The boy was amazed at the old man's answer. Peter said in amazement, "How did you know what I was thinking?"

Mr Heaven replied, "I am able to read people's thoughts and I dislike dishonest people. Be honest from now on, Peter."

In horror the school boy rushed out of the café, for he suddenly realised who Mr Heaven really was and also the meeting in the café was no accident.

The following day Peter went back to the Melbourne café to see if he could find Mr Heaven. Abraham Heaven was sitting at the same table drinking tea and reading a newspaper. The boy went up to him and gave him a card. Inside the card was written:

Dear Heavenly Father
You are indeed very special, from now on I shall respect you.
Regards, St Peter

A few months earlier in Heaven, St Peter and God had had an argument. In anger, God had turned St Peter into the Melbourne school boy and placed him on Earth until he apologized to God.

The Mexican Good Omen Birthday Cake

It was a boiling hot day in Mexico City, the capital of Mexico. Pedro Guadalajara was the Head Cleaner at St Lucas Catholic Church; he took great care in keeping St Lucas Catholic Church in excellent condition.

Pedro and his wife Maria had fifteen children, the family were very poor but in good health and very happy.

Pedro had been saving for over five months to buy a birthday cake for her fifteenth child Enrico. Mr and Mrs Guadalajara wanted to order a cake from Golden Cakes City Store. Only the very rich shopped at that store, but that was not going to prevent Pedro and Maria from ordering a cake.

The following day Mr and Mrs Guadalajara went to Golden Cakes City Store. The moment they entered the shop, the Manager Mr Extra Tampiro rushed up to them for he was rather embarrassed to have poor people in his exclusive shop. The couple were clean but badly dressed. Pedro had on a pair of work boots, a torn shirt and a pair of beach-wear shorts. Maria wore a very low-cut blouse, and one of her daughter's mini skirts, and she had had her hair coloured in a light shade of blue. The couple looked a terrible mess.

Mr Tampiro smiled and tried not to grin at the couple. In a very quiet pleasant voice he said to them, "The Good Luck Cakes Shop is further down the road." The Good Luck Cakes Shop was a less expensive cake shop. The business was run by St Vincent's de Paul Catholic Church organisation, the food was very cheap and well prepared. The couple were furious. Maria said in a very loud voice, "My husband has saved for over five months to buy a birthday cake for our child Enrico's ninth birthday. Do you think, Mr Tampiro, that the rich are gods that you must obey?"

Mr Tampiro quickly took the order without saying a word. A week later a magnificent birthday cake was delivered to the Guadalajara's residence. Enrico was very excited and so were the rest of the family. Enrico quickly ripped open the birthday cake envelope and as he did so a small piece of paper fell to the floor. He picked it up and gave the paper to his mother. For a few seconds Maria could not believe her eyes, for it was cheque in US dollars – it read 25 million dollars! Attached to the cheque was a letter, the letter said a gift from Count Henri Lebon, Switzerland.

On the day that Mr and Mrs Guadalajara had gone to Golden Cakes City Store a billionaire was also in the shop, Count Henri Lebon. He was in his late forties and was on holiday from Switzerland. For some time he had wanted to live in Mexico due to the warm climate and own a business, but still kept his chateau in Switzerland. Golden Cakes City Store was just the ideal shop located in the heart of Mexico City. Henri Lebon also wanted to do something worthwhile with his life. He wanted to help the very poor, funds from every cake sold from his shop would be given to charity. Also the Count loved to bake cakes. Over time he became world famous for the beautiful cake designs he invented.

The sale of the shop had been very successful. Mr Tampiro was delighted to receive 30 million US dollars for his shop. Now, finally, he could retire and travel the world.

Six months earlier one of Mr Tampiro's customers, a well known clairvoyant named Mme Venuslode came one afternoon into the cake shop to tell Extra Tampiro a very strange tale about a dream that she had had the previous night. In her dream an angel had appeared to her – Angel Quideoeous. The angel had told her that Golden Cakes City Store would be sold within six months to a nobleman with the initials H.L. and that a poor couple would also be given a huge sum of money from the nobleman, which would of course enable the couple with their fifteen children to have better lifestyle.

Mr Tampiro had considered the prediction utter rubbish!

It is said that God works in mysterious ways and indeed that is true.

Wi, Wi, Won

Once upon a time in a land named Worth, lived an oriental man named Wi Wi Won, Wi for short. He wanted to travel the world, but at the age of 101 he thought that he had left his wish too late.

One day a merchant came to his door, the merchant showed Wi many interesting colourful items for the house – a broomstick that could fold, a lemon scented like an orange, wooden shoes that could fold, but suddenly Wi noticed a statue made of matchsticks. The statue was named Destiny, whatever its owner wished would come true, but there were conditions, regulations had to be observed, the tests that were taught, no short cuts to gain wealth etc. Wi immediately purchased the statue of Destiny, and the merchant told Wi he would gain what he wanted within six months, but for the rest of his life he was required to help others in need, otherwise his wish would not come true.

The merchant was an ex-criminal, and while he was a criminal he worked for the underworld, a place of great crime. He sold drugs and, to avoid the law, he lived life on the run. One day he came across a priest, the priest helped him change his ways and to assist people in need, the merchant made good luck statues from matchsticks and named these statues Destiny.

Funds raised from the sale of the statues were given to a variety of charities in the land of Worth, and also throughout the world. And as for Wi Wi Won, his wish came true – he travelled the world.

Free Trip to the Moon

"All aboard," shouted the Sydney Trainair express driver Mr Rael Roadtrack, "We are off to the moon in five minutes." Excited passengers rushed to their seats and waited with great excitement for the trip of a lifetime to begin. In fact they had waited five years to purchase tickets to the moon, the waiting list was very, very long and it increased year after year.

Thousands of people in Australia and all over the world were desperate to visit the moon. One of the many moon regulations was that none of the passengers were allowed to walk on the moon because none of the passengers were trained astronauts.

The Trainair express is both a train and an aircraft. As a train it only goes to local places, and twice a week as a plane it goes to the moon.

One evening, Mr Roadtrack received a very unusual telephone call from a Mr Ravi Singhmonie II who claimed to be a multi-millionaire and an owner of a hotel in Delhi, India. Ravi said that he was on holiday in Australia for a few days and that the following day it was his birthday so he wanted to celebrate his birthday in great style by visiting the moon without having to wait approximately five years to go on the trip and if Rael gave him a ticket, Ravi would give him a thank you gift of a million dollars. Mr Roadtrack immediately agreed to the request. After all, who often comes across a multi-millionaire willing to part with a million dollars to celebrate his birthday in great style?

The following day Ravi arrived at the Trainair express station two minutes before the trip began. Rael rushed up to Ravi and gave him a birthday present, a very expensive bottle of champagne. Ravi grabbed the bottle of champagne and promised Rael his reward after the trip.

The trip to the moon took longer than expected due to some engine trouble. It took over six hours to get to the moon. Usually it took two and a half hours for the Trainair express to land on the moon. That afternoon the moon was very dark. A storm had occurred, but the storm only lasted a few minutes and then suddenly the moon shone very, very brightly. In fact the light was so bright it was very difficult to see anything for most of the trip.

Stories about hidden treasure on the moon in a cave were often spoken about by people that had been on a trip. Ravi and some other passengers had no interest in taking photographs and enjoying the scenery. So he, with several other men, tried to break the Trainair express doors and windows so that they could get on the moon and search for the hidden treasure. The task was impossible for the doors were made of steel and the windows were break-proof.

After a few minutes trying to break the doors and the windows they gave up and sat down very disappointed and were forced to look at the moon!

The other passengers were so enjoying taking photographs that they had not noticed what Ravi and the other men were trying to do, for the men were very careful not to distract people otherwise the passengers would have contacted Rael and the journey would have ended.

The hours went by slowly. Seventeen hours later Mr Roadtrack landed the Trainair on Earth. He then rushed into the crowd to find Mr Singhmonie II, but Ravi had escaped by getting into a huge crate full of tins of sardines that was going by rail to Queensland.

Two days later Ravi arrived in Queensland very tired and stinking of sardines! He went to a very expensive hotel and told the hotel manager that he was an Indian prince that had come to Australia on a business trip and had had his passport and luggage stolen at Sydney Airport. Then he was thrown into a huge crate full of tins of sardines that was going by rail to Queensland and two days later he found himself on the Gold Coast, Queensland. The hotel manager took pity on him and gave Ravi first-class hotel accommodation, meals, beautiful clothes, a very nice pair of Australian leather shoes, $5,000 pocket money and a first-class airline ticket back to Sydney. Ravi could not believe his luck!

As for Mr Roadtrack he resigned from his job and travelled all over Australia looking for Ravi Singhmonie II.

Over the years both men continued to be dishonest until they were finally caught by the police, now both men work for their local council as gardeners.

The moral of the story is think before you are dishonest, for it is not worth it.

Seychelles Peak

On the island of Seychelles in the Indian Ocean lived a large blue bird named Seychelles Peak, Peak for short, who could speak three human languages – Hindustani, French and English. Peak had a wish he wanted to work as an actor in Hollywood, Los Angeles in America, then the other birds would stop laughing at him about his wish. "Fancy this and fancy that" they named Peak.

As Seychelles is thousands of miles away from America, Peak would have to exercise on a daily basis for several months to get fit to fly to Los Angeles. The flying exercise would start off for two hours, and as the days went by increased the hours of training until Peak could cope with the long hours of flying to America.

Most years Seychelles and the surrounding islands had cyclones, strong storms with plenty of rain and wind, ideal weather to fly to America. Peak would arrive in Los Angeles quicker with the aid of a cyclone. The following year in February a cyclone occurred (usually cyclones happen early each year), and because of the cyclone the flying trip to America took two days, six hours and half a minute to arrive on a sunny Sunday afternoon in Los Angeles. The flying trip usually takes one week, ten hours and one minute, which Seychelles Peak did some years ago but ended up in Peru!

A famous actor was rushing around being filmed, when all of a sudden the actor looked up into the sky because he could hear a loud noise – the flapping of bird's wings – and saw Seychelles Peak flying full speed towards him. Peak was shouting with joy "Hello friend, I'm Seychelles Peak from the Indian Ocean island of Seychelles and I have come to take part in your film this afternoon."

The following year Seychelles Peak won Best Actor Award and Peru invited Peak to celebrate his win with them in great style; firstly he was flown to Peru, then given a huge reception which went on for days.

Seychelles Peak continued with his acting career until he was too old to continue working, he then went back to the Seychelles to retire and live in great style and as for the birds that had laughed at him, they came to respect him.

Rodriguez Island's Best Dog

Rodriguez Island is part of Mauritius Island, though several hundred miles from each other. Rodriguez has beautiful beaches, good fishing due to the Indian Ocean and mostly fine weather all the year round.

On the island lived a bad man named Jacques Bon Jour, at night he stole neighbourhood dogs. He did not really like dogs, but Jacques was a poor man and he got a good income from stealing the dogs. He only stole valuable dogs from the rich on the island and sold them to rich families on the neighbouring islands, Seychelles, Mauritius and La Reunion. On Jacque's day off from stealing dogs, he would go fishing and hope to catch a fish for his supper. The Indian Ocean has a variety of fish like the Blue Marlin (which is a large fish and often in Mauritius a Blue Marlin contest takes place) to the tiny fish like the Sardine, also large red crabs and tiny to large King Prawns can be caught.

Jacques would cook his meals on a primus rather like a small stove but without gas or electricity. The appliance would have oil placed inside it, then lit with a match like a gas stove, and he would cook seafood meals outside his cottage due to the strong smell.

One night Jacques stole a white dog, named White Dog by his British owner because the dog was a large, beautiful, intelligent, white long-haired dog from Europe and the only white long-haired dog on the island.

Bon Jour got to know the owner's gardener, and this was an opportunity for him to ask questions about the owner and the dog. The gardener was a good man but not very intelligent to understand what was really being asked, but he answered all the important questions that Bon Jour needed to know to enable him to be successful in stealing White Dog.

White Dog had a huge beautiful kennel (a dog house) at the back of the magnificent mansion near the swimming pool, and he had the best lifestyle for a dog. Every six months he and his master went to live in Britain. Walter, the owner, owned a clothing factory and a lovely house in the capital of Wales, Cardiff.

Each night at 8 pm White Dog would be brought inside the mansion for the night; the dog even had his own bedroom with a large blue and gold dog bed and nice blue and gold curtains at his bedroom windows. One evening at about 6 pm, Jacques stole White Dog, the dog was terrified for it knew its fate, as it had a god-given gift – it could see into the future and its future now was not looking good, unless it did something fast to escape.

On that fateful night Jacques grabbed White Dog and pushed the frightened dog into a huge bag with a long zip and immediately zipped the bag up, then carried the heavy bag back to his old wooden house in the woods.

The bag was not very strong, it was made of plastic and had several small holes which White Dog scratched until he had made a huge hole to escape later, but before he escaped he let Jacques carry him – a huge weight of a dog, that would be the first punishment, the second punishment would come later.

The moment Jacques got home, he threw down the heavy bag. Poor White Dog, he ended up with a few bruises, then Jacques went inside his house to rest.

White Dog soon got out of the hole in the bag and quickly went to fetch stones and wood to place inside the bag through the large hole, so that Jacques would think that the dog was still inside the bag. White Dog worked as fast as he could and was able to run at full speed back to his kind master before 8 pm.

A few hours had passed and Jacques went outside to fetch the bag to put White Dog in a large cage which was inside the wooden cottage, but as he unzipped the bag a little to look at the dog, all he could see were stones and pieces of wood – no dog! Frantically he unzipped the bag fully, shocked and thinking how could a large dog escape and who had filled the bag with stones and wood? Unless the dog had been stolen by one of his neighbours, then he saw the large hole in the bag.

Jacques was so scared of the police, the following day he left Rodriguez on the first boat to the Seychelles, never to return to his home.

The White Dog fantasy story is from a terrible true story about dogs being cruelly treated by their owner, in Melbourne Australia. The Melbourne newspaper, *The Age*, on the 3rd February 2012 reported that authorities rescued many dogs from their cruel owner – one of the dogs was a beautiful intelligent white dog, a short-haired dog, which was living in a cage too small for the animal to stand up.

It is in his honour that I wrote this fantasy story 'White Dog' about such brave dogs.

Vive! La Reunion

Bon Jour La Reunion.

La Reunion is another island in the Indian Ocean below Mauritius, further away from the Seychelles and Rodriguez islands. A nice group of islands Mauritius, Seychelles and Rodriguez are independent, La Reunion belongs to France, St Denis is the capital and this is where the Tournés family live – this is their story of good luck that suddenly came to them in 1968.

In St Denis at La Reunion Museum is a Spanish treasure, this treasure gave the Tournés family a better lifestyle. Long ago tall ships came to the islands, carrying a variety of merchandise which consisted of spices like curry powder, foods like beans, red kidney beans, flour to make bread, pies and cakes, cooking oil, leather goods, woollen carpets, silks from china, cotton and linen materials from India. Also gold and silver jewellery; large diamonds that sparkle in the sun; pale and dark green oriental jade – magnificent and brings good fortune to the wearer; bright red rubies, large like cherries; and gold coins that also sparkle. With such wealthy cargo on the seas this would attract bad men, pirates, they would sail the seas looking to steal from ships, they would attack the crew and burn the cargo ships to gain control of the wealth. Even today several sunken ships and some of their goods still surround the islands.

In 1968 schoolboys, Pierre Tournés, and his brother Jean-Claude found a sixteenth-century wooden trunk full of Spanish jewellery and many bags of gold coins while underwater swimming.

Most weekends Pierre and Jean-Claude would catch the local bus to take them to the seaside and one warm afternoon their lives would change for the better for they would become wealthy and famous. Their mother, Rose-Noelle, was a widow in her forties and worked as a primary school teacher, her wages just helped all three of them to get by. Pierre and Jean-Claude were form VI students and the following year they hoped to go to France to study at Paris University, it would be a dream come true for them.

Most weekends the boys would catch the local bus to the beach – they loved the sea air, the seagulls, the fishing boats, they even had a few fishermen friends and often they would take home fresh fish, gifts from the fishermen for Mme Tournés to cook. Most Sundays she would cook a delicious poisson (fish) soufflé and make a tasty tomato and onion chutney to compliment the fish meal. On that fateful day in 1968, the boys quickly ate their toast and fried eggs for breakfast and drank cups of tea before dashing down the road to catch the first bus to the seaside – the 7.30 a.m. bus. The bus ride took twenty minutes to get to the beach, and that day the weather was warm with a clear blue sky, perfect weather to swim in the calm ocean.

Pierre and Jean-Claude liked underwater swimming for it was a different world, full of magic, a world of magnificent colours, they loved to see the pretty yellow, pink, blue and black and white spotted fish swim past them, the pale orange and white coral and the black odd-looking eels that swam amongst the bright green seaweed.

On their special day the boys were enjoying underwater swimming, when suddenly Pierre started shouting with excitement and pointed to something that looked like a box. The boys quickly swam towards the box which was a very old wooden trunk, half hidden underneath a big orange coral and eels sat on it. The boys frantically tried to open the trunk with a large piece of coral, for several minutes, they struggled, no luck!

For about a month they would go underwater swimming to have a look at the trunk and try desperately to open it, they then decided to tell La Reunion Museum in St Denis, and soon the local media were on the beach reporting the good news to the world.

When the trunk was removed from the sea and opened at La Reunion Museum, Spanish gold and silver jewellery, diamonds, jade and rubies and dozens of bags of Spanish gold coins were discovered, sixteenth-century wealth. The sudden good fortune for the Tournés family enabled them to have better lives and also help their relatives, Rose-Noelle retire from teaching after thirty-five years, Pierre and Jean-Claude were able to go to Paris University.

Five years had passed, Pierre and Jean-Claude returned to La Reunion with their hotel management degrees and open a restaurant in St Denis and put some of the Spanish coins on display for their customers to admire.

Rose-Noelle's fish soufflé recipe was greatly enjoyed by their customers and this is the recipe:

Poisson Soufflé

Ingredients:

3 lbs red fish or any large fish
½ lemon, sliced
2 bay leaves, 1 pinch thyme
Salt and pepper to taste
2 cloves garlic
1 tablespoon butter
1 tablespoon flour,
½ cup milk
3 egg whites, well beaten
2 tablespoons minced parsley
2 tablespoons lemon juice
Breadcrumbs

Method:

- Put the fish in a deep pan and cover with water. Add salt, pepper, lemon, bay leaves, thyme and garlic to the water in which the fish is boiling. Cook the fish until done, about twenty minutes.

- Remove from water and take off the skin and bones and flake the fish.

- Put the butter in a saucepan and add flour and a little milk. Add minced parsley and cook for about five minutes, then add flaked fish when well blended, take off the fire and add two teaspoons of lemon juice.

- Stir well and add beaten whites of eggs. Put in a buttered casserole, sprinkle with breadcrumbs and put a little melted butter on top.

- Put the casserole in another vessel of hot water and bake for 15 minutes.

La Reunion

Island of French Culture

The Capital
St. Denis

Indian Ocean

Tim Vaneca-Dumas

PEGLAND

Peg Characters Information:

Mr 21st Century Pegg is about 50 years old. He likes to smoke a pipe. The pipe is shaped like a star. It was purchased while on a trip to Starland.

Mrs 21st Century Pegg is about 40 years old. She likes to dress well and she likes silk and linen clothes and also huge earrings.

Mr Will Do Peg is about 40 years old. He likes fancy ties and 60's designer clothes.

Mr Wild Do Peg is about 46 years old. He likes to dress 'wild' and grows his hair very long but keeps his hair tidy with huge hairclips shaped like giant ears.

King Star 1 is about 60 years old. He likes William Shakespeare plays, so likes to dress like one of William Shakespeare's characters in one of his plays.

Once upon a time in a beautiful South Pacific Ocean country named Pegland lived Mr and Mrs 21st Century Pegg. Mr 21st Century Pegg was a small peg but a very strong peg. He liked to care for his beautiful garden and Mrs 21st Century Pegg loved to bake little peg-shaped chocolate cakes.

Their lives were filled with nothing but happiness, and their neighbours always dropped in to tell them the latest happy news, but for some weeks happy news suddenly stopped.

One day a neighbour Mr Will Do Peg came to visit them and told them a very sad story. The local primary school needed to be painted before the annual peg flower show and the Head Master, Mr Wild Do Peg did not have extra funds to buy paint.

Some days passed and Mr Will Do Peg held a meeting at the Silver and Gold Town Hall. Every peg – two hundred pegs only in Pegland – attended the meeting and helped raise funds for St Peg School by making and selling little peg-shaped chocolate cakes to hospitals, and schools and also to a country close by named Starland.

Starland is bigger and richer than Pegland and it has its own King – King Star 1. The King was delighted with the peg-shaped chocolate cakes and bought as many chocolate cakes as possible.

St Peg School was painted on time and the annual Peg Flower Show was a great success, and so Pegland became very happy again.

STARLAND

Ratt used to live in a bottle shop inside a very small box. He had an ambition to have a better lifestyle, so he decided to live at the Prime Minister's House in Pegland.

The Prime Minister of Pegland hated rats but knew that Ratt would make a great pet. The Prime Minister also knew that Prince Elbee of Starland liked unusual animals and so Ratt was sent by boat to Starland as a gift from the Prime Minister of Pegland to the Starland royal family.

Ratt was delighted with his new lifestyle for he had always wanted to live well and so the adventures of Ratt would start… but that would be for next time.

This is the story of how Ratt became a royal pet. In Ratt's new privileged position he found the opportunity to make some new friends who were known as Ratt Ratti Comeboy and You You Ratt.

You You used to live in a gutter before he lived with the Bishop of Starland. For several days You You would stand outside Bishop Hi Pi Onion's residence and shout, "Let me in for I am a homeless rat."

Is that an example of a good Christian? Why ignore a poor rat in need?

The bishop was amazed at the rat's determination and decided to let You You inside the house, give him a meal and then get rid of him.

Unfortunately the Bishop's plan did not work out, for You You refused to leave the residence. So, after a few minutes of running around the dining room the tired Bishop gave in to You You and they became good friends a few weeks later.

Then one day they heard that St Better Church where Bishop Hi Pi Opinion gave Sunday services was going to celebrate Bishop Onion's 76th birthday. The whole town came alive with the news and that is how Ratt and You You met – at the Bishop's birthday party.

A year had passed and by now both rats were enjoying their new lifestyles. And so let us leave Ratt and You You for some other time...

INFORMATION ON THE STARLAND ROYAL FAMILY

King Do Star Do Teff is about 60 years old. He is a part-time farmer and likes looking after the Silver Forest, the only forest in Starland. Queen Der Yellow- Rose Do Teff is about 45 years old.

Twenty years earlier Queen Der 1 met King Star 1 at a New Year dinner dance and two years later the couple got married.

Prince Elbee Do Nur Do Teff is 17 years old. He has no interest in being a prince. He would prefer to be a musician playing wild jungle music!

Princess Pinn Do Mee Do Teff is 14 years old. She enjoys going to the local secondary school and takes part in school plays and hopes some day to have her own drama school.

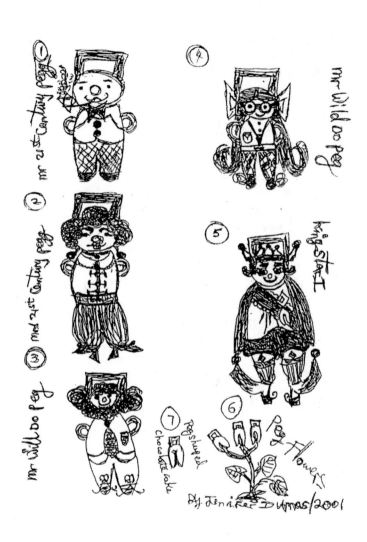

1. mr 21st Century pegg
2. mrs 21st Century pegg
3. mr Will Do Peg
4. mr Will Do Peg
5. king star I
6. Peg Flowers
7. Peg shaped chocolate

By Jennifer Dumas/2001

28

Star land
Peg characters
⑥

Queen Her I
Yellow-Rose.
Maiden Name: Pegg-Pegg
Married Syrname & Do TEFF

⑦

Prince Flee III
Do N.W.   Do
Syrname: TEFF

⑧

Princess
Ann Domee
Syrname
Do Teff

Ratt Rattii Comedy
the Sash re-
presents the
royal
Starland
household.

You-You Ratt

29

The Prime Minister of England Year
Mr Association Harvest Pegg

The eyepatch is due to an ac-
-cident with a pen, so P.M has
only one eye.

Mr Association Harvest Pegg
is about 47 years old, he likes
dressing in the 70's style
and loves cats, he has three
cats.

The P.M is single and
likes to travel and enjoy
50s and 60s music.

Bishop Hi Pi Onion Age: 75.
Hi Pi is very proud of his huge
eye brows and refuses to cut them
off.
Bishop Onion has a fine singing
voice and likes to sing at parties

The Island of Vizo in the Indian Ocean

Once upon a time a robot named Mr Addam U lived on the island of Vizo.

Mr U loved cats. He had 50 white female cats and 50 black male cats. Mr U's cats were all vegetarian. They only ate chocolate ice-cream and chocolate cake.

Mr Addam U is a mechanical toy robot. He was made in America and brought to Vizo by a rich businessman who opened the one and only restaurant on the island named Hi! Restaurant.

Mr U loved the island and the restaurant, but after five years working in the restaurant decided to retire.

Each day Mr U would meet his Maori friend Mr Rosehop Johns who is a musician at Hi! Restaurant.

Mr Rosehip Johns is a Maori a native of New Zealand. Many Maori men own fishing boats; six years ago while out fishing in Wellington a storm occurred and after two weeks at sea Rosehip landed on the Island of Vizo. He loved the island and decided to make Vizo his new home, but still he felt homesick for New Zealand, so every Christmas he would set sail for New Zealand to visit his parents, five brothers, two sisters and his two pet chickens that live in Wellington.

Each year Mr U and Mr Johns hold an annual party at Hi! Restaurant to raise funds for the island's economy, for Vizo Island is only five miles long and ten miles wide and being so small requires funds from neighbouring islands to survive.

The main crop on Vizo is corn, other crops are sugar cane and pineapples. Most of the crops are exported to other islands, one of the lands being Susu Island, the sister island to Vizo Island.

The King of Susu Island usually gives a big annual donation but forgot to send his annual donation. Within hours the sad news spread across Vizo Island. The Vizorians were very upset. Several Vizorians contacted Mr U and Mr Johns. Mr U can sing and Mr Johns can play the flute and also sing to hold concerts to raise funds for the Island's economy.

Over many weeks Mr U and Mr Johns held concerts, and happily Vizo Island was given more donations than usual because news spread across the world about this wonderful little island in the Indian Ocean.

Mr U and Mr Johns' music can be heard on Saturday afternoons on Y-U-H-E-A-R Vizo Radio.

True:

A Maori is a native of New Zealand.

New Zealand has two islands, North Island and South Island.

Wellington is the capital of New Zealand.

A robot is a mechanical toy.

A vegetarian is a person or animal that does not eat meat.

Vizo Island is a fairyland island.

Seychelles

Seychelles is made up of
many small islands, the biggest of which is
Mahé.

Indian Ocean

Indian Ocean

Mahé ISLAND

This Drawing incorporates
montages of the
many different parts
but I am trying my grand
best to remind you
of the many parts
you will find in this
enchanted mahouses.

Indian
Ocean

The
Victoria
market.

Indian
Ocean

J. M. Vignes-Dumas
2012

Welcome From Vignes family

Giant Golden Delight Flowers
on the Island of Seychelles in the Indian Ocean

Once upon a time on the Island of Seychelles lived a huge flower, in fact a giant flower. It had a beautiful perfume rather like fresh lemons and had two colours on its petals, bright yellow and bright pink. The colour pink represents the female flower. Not often seen nor found are the male flowers with yellow and blue petals. The colour blue represents the male flower.

The locals named the beautiful female flower Giant Golden Delight, for each day near sunset the flower glowed magnificent yellow and pink rays of light (the colours of the petals rather look like firecracker lights).

Millionaire tourist Mr 'Gogo' George Bell Pime II is about 60 years old. He is a native American who likes to wear huge African bells on chains attached by huge hairpins to his head. Bells bring good luck and that is why George is known as 'Gogo' due to the sound of the bells.

One day Gogo from the island Mauritius, the neighbouring island near Seychelles island, visited the giant flower and decided to purchase it and offered a huge price to the Seychelles government. But the government would not sell their unique flower, for Giant Golden Delight helped the island's tourist industry to prosper. Each year thousands of people from all over the world came to the island to visit the beautiful flower.

Five years went by and Gogo returned to Seychelles Island and this time he brought with him a small Giant Golden Delight male flower. It takes ten years for the flower to grow about twenty foot high. Over the years many male and female Giant Golden Delights grew on both islands.

True:

Mauitius Island and Seychelles Island – both islands can be found near the African continent.

A native American is a person of non-European race.

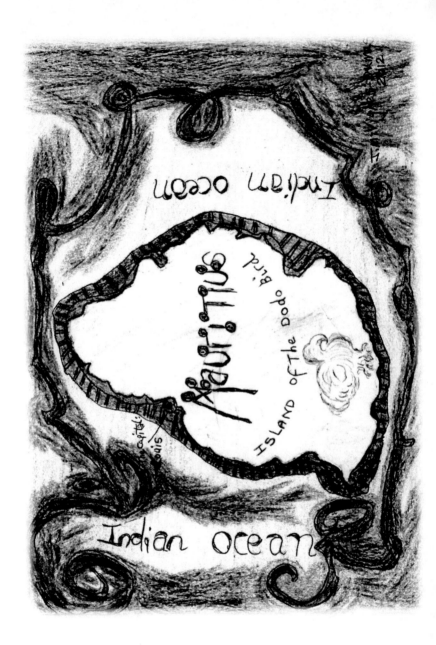

The Dodo Bird
that Escaped from Danger to Freedom

Once upon a time on the island of Mauritius lived a Dodo bird. The birds were very large and due to their weight were unable to fly.

All types of birds and other animals lived a happy and peaceful life in the island's forests. In one of the forests lived a Dodo bird named Mr Mauritius (Maurie to his friends). He was most unusual looking. He had one orange leg and one pink leg. He would proudly show off his legs and say, "I am special and some day I shall be remembered as the multi-coloured Dodo bird that lived on a small island in the Indian Ocean."

Some years passed and two businessmen from Britain came to the island to study plants, especially the coconut tree. The men planned to plant coconut trees in Britain in a greenhouse, sell coconut juice and make a fortune.

When the men arrived by boat on the island, Maurie happened to be asleep under a coconut tree, when suddenly he woke up with a fright. He could hear human voices. He knew that the voices were human because years ago his dear mother Lala was caught by several men and he never saw his mother again.

Now Maurie was very scared again for he did not want to get caught like his mother. He got up and ran as fast as possible behind a bush to hide from the humans. The humans got nearer and nearer. Maurie was trying to stay calm but fainted. When he woke up he was face to face with two men. The men had placed him on a huge sheet and had tied his legs together with rope. They were looking over Maurie and were discussing how they were going to take him to Britain with them. Poor Maurie was terrified and pretended to be asleep.

The hours passed slowly and now it was night time, by now Maurie was desperate to go home. He was thinking of a plan on how he was going to escape, while all this time his best friend – a pigeon named Mr Pee – had been sitting on a branch above Maurie. Mr Pee had seen everything and was also thinking how he was going to help Maurie escape. The men were getting ready to go to sleep in their boat and this was an opportunity not to be missed to escape. Mr Pee flew off the branch and landed gently on Maurie's back. "Wake up my friend," said Mr Pee in rather a loud whisper, "I have found a piece of rock to cut the rope." Maurie placed the piece of rock in his mouth and rubbed it as hard as possible against the rope. A few minutes passed. The rope snapped and Maurie was free.

The happy news is that Mr Pee and Mr Mauritius escaped in the night and as for the two men they went back to Britain very disappointed with their trip because they had been fooled by a bird!

The men were planning to do something dishonest, steal a very rare bird, sell it and make a fortune.

True:

Mauritius can be found near the African continent.

A greenhouse is a glass house made specially to house and grow delicate and/or tropical plants that need extra care to grow.

A Dodo bird is a huge flightless bird.

A Pigeon bird is a very small bird that can fly.

The Dodo Bird.

Mr Bee

Colour Orange

the colour of the feather grey and white

Colour Dark brown light brown Colour

the Dodo bird Named W6 Mauritius

Colour Pink

Colour Pink

← The colours Required for the Dodo Bird.

Courage – China 1885

Once upon a time in China lived a wild tiger, a cat with two heads. The cat belonged to Emperor Lui Hui Fatt II. The Emperor was about 100 years old but due to his excellent health he looked much younger.

Emperor Lui had a magnificent palace but preferred the outdoor life. He lived in a very small cave above his palace with his pet tiger named Two-Heads. Two-Heads had lived on the African continent in a small country named Kenya where many magnificent and unusual animals can be found – for example the giraffe, a tall animal with a long neck.

Two-Heads was a gift from the Prime Minister of Kenya on the occasion of the Emperor's 100th birthday. Two-Heads was not only good looking but a genius cat and the only tiger in the world that could read and speak human languages. He loved the beautiful Chinese high-class dialect Mandarin. In fact each day Two-Heads would read the China Daily Newspaper to Emperor Lui, for the Emperor's eyesight was not very good due to his age.

One day Two-Heads was reading the newspaper when all of a sudden he saw a very interesting advertisement. It mentioned a miracle eye medication made from tropical flowers and honey. The medication was made on a very small island above the Fijian Islands in the South Pacific Ocean. Tuvalu Island has magnificent white sands, a good fishing industry and lovely tropical flowers. Juices from the tropical flowers and honey made the eyes stronger, and no eye disease would infect the eyes again as soon as the medication was placed on the eyes.

The Emperor purchased the eye medication and was able to see clearly instantly.

Two-Heads had given Emperor Lui faith to believe in an unusual eye medication that would restore his eyes, and due to the wonderful love between a tiger and a very old man Two-Heads became a national mascot (mascot – person, animal or object regarded as a luck omen) for people all over the world.

True:

The island of Tuvalu is above the Fijian islands in the South Pacific Ocean.

1906 China

Once upon a time in 1906 China lived an Emperor named Chenxu. He was about 43 years old and very artistic. He had painted his palace blue and gold. He also made wooden furniture for charities. The funds from the sale of the furniture were given to sick children that lived in villages miles away from the nearest hospital in China.

Emperor Chenxu enjoyed making wooden furniture for charities and took his royal duties very seriously, but he had a wish. He wanted to stop doing royal duties for a few months and travel around the world, write reports about his travels, then return to China to continue his royal duties.

One day the Emperor was walking near the palace kitchen when all of a sudden the palace cook threw an empty herb container out of the kitchen window. The cook had not noticed the Emperor, otherwise he would not have done such a thing, for it is very untidy to throw out unwanted items in the garden and on the street. Chenxu picked up the wooden box and then thought, "I shall write down my wish, then place my wish inside this box and just for fun place it inside the palace pond and perhaps my wish will come true."

Chenxu then rushed to his study and quickly wrote down his wish on a piece of paper, placed his wish inside the box, then rushed out of his study walking fast towards the palace pond. Before he could reach the pond the Emperor heard his name being called. He turned around to see who was calling him. It was his brother Prince Hui Lu Hong. Chenxu quickly threw the box into the pond. The little container landed on a frog's head! Mr Lee Lu Fatt, the frog, was furious for he was having his lunch and did not like to be disturbed while eating. "What is this?" he said shouting. He pulled open the lid and took out the piece of paper. "Fantastic, and I cannot read!" said Lee Lu in a sarcastic voice. "I shall take the paper to my cousin Hung Fatt." Re-named Go Leap by his British doctor owner Dr William Mushroom, Hung Fatt was renamed Go Leap because he could jump very high off the ground.

Dr William Mushroom lived in a small two-roomed flat above a sweet shop. The rooms were filled with boxes containing books, maps, piles of documents, laboratory instruments, a large bed, a cot for Go Leap, one small wardrobe, one chair, a desk, a kitchen sink, a stove and a stool.

Dr Mushroom was about 65 years old. He had spent 18 years in China doing research on insect behaviour. His father, Sir Peter Mushroom, had given him a cottage in Cornwall, England, and every 2–3 years the doctor would go by ship to the UK and would spend 3–4 months in the cottage in Cornwall. He would take Go Leap with him. Go Leap had been taught to read and write the Chinese dialect Mandarin and the English language. Go Leap was a friend and assistant to Dr Mushroom.

At exactly two o'clock, Lee Lu arrived at Dr Mushroom's residence. He tapped at the front door. William Mushroom answered the door. He was delighted to see Lee Lu. "Come in!" he shouted with delight. "Go Leap is eating a lychee, would you like a lychee?"

"No thank you," said Lee Lu, "but I shall take some lychees home with me if that is alright?"

"Fine," said the doctor, smiling.

Go Leap came into the room. Lee Lu handed him the piece of paper and for a few seconds Go Leap studied the paper, then said in rather an important voice, "It would seem that Emperor Chenxu is disappointed in his lifestyle."

"Well I never!" said the doctor in amazement.

Lee Lu was in too much of a shock to say anything.

William Mushroom thought for a while. "How about a plan?"

"A plan?" said the frogs, in shock.

When William Mushroom told Chenxu about his idea, the Emperor was delighted. The plan was to travel with the doctor, Go Leap and Lee Lu to Britain every 2–3 years.

True

China, East Asia.

Lychee, a fruit grown in tropical countries and islands.

Fairyland names – Emperor Chenxu, Prince Hui Lu Hong

The Adventures of Pongkipui the Piglet

Pongkipui was the only piglet of Mr and Mrs Pigton. They lived on a small island named Pig Island in the Pacific Ocean. No humans lived on the island, only pigs and wild birds. The island was magnificent – white sand, beautiful tropical flowers and fruit trees. Pig Island was only 10 miles by 14 miles long, and due to its very small size it was not yet a tourist attraction.

Mr and Mrs Pigton were wealthy pigs, they owned the only supermarket on the island. On Pongkipui's eighteenth birthday he received a beautiful motorbike from his parents. With great excitement he immediately jumped onto the bike, and rode at full speed to his best friend's house. But, on the way to his best friend's house Pongkipui was suddenly forced to make a desperate decision – slow down or continue the speed, for now he was in between two huge trucks. Pongkipui desperately tried to overtake the front truck, however the truck driver Mr Pigey would not reduce the speed of the truck for he was furious that a motorbike rider was trying to overtake him. The situation was hopeless. Nor would the second truck driver, Mr Hogg, give in to let Pongkipui overtake him, for he was already very late with the stock for the pig lot factory.

Pongkipui desperately tried overtaking the first truck but the situation got worse. He then had to make a terrible decision. He had to let go of his motorbike and jump onto the first truck to save his life. The motorbike was completely crushed by Mr Hogg's truck but Pongkipui's life had been saved.

A few months had passed and Pongkipui's parents purchased another motorbike for him. The moment that the motorbike was delivered to the Pigton's home Pongkipui jumped onto it and rode at full speed to his best friend's home. Suddenly the bike lost control and Pongkipui, still on his bike, landed up a tree! Again Pongkipui's life had been saved.

Over the years Pongkipui became a champion motorbike rider. He took part in many local and international motorbike competitions, and in 1965 in France at the Annual French Motorbike International Contest Pongkipui was voted Mr International Best Rider for 1965.

The Tale of the Missing Necklace
on the Island Named Magic

Once upon a time on the island of Magic in the Indian Ocean lived three cats – Sonny-pink Whisker her two kittens Baby Puss I and Baby Puss II. Mr Whisker lived on the neighbouring island, Highgrade Island for business reasons. He helped run a glass jar factory – there were only two factories on the island, glass jars and wooden boxes were produced. The products were sent to Magic Island.

Magic Island.

Sonny-pink, BabyPuss I and Baby Puss II lived in a forest named Grass Hopper, so called due to the many grasshoppers that lived in that forest.

On Magic Island only animals lived, also four different fruits grew – strawberries, apples, bananas and plums – plus hundreds of acres of pine trees and other varieties of trees.

The Whisker family had two grasshopper friends, Mr Cow and Mr Beck. They liked to make jams. 60% of the funds from the sale of the jams went to the local hospital, 20% of the funds went to Highgrade Island to purchase glass jars and wooden boxes for the jams. The jam was exported by boat to all surrounding islands and the remaining 20% of the funds was for Mr Cow and Mr Beck's wages.

Magic Island had no human nation and no currency-paper money so shells were used as currency. They were known as To-to Lu Lot. They were pink and white coloured and were heart-shaped. Heart-shaped items attract good fortune and indeed orders for the jams were so many that Mr Cow and Mr Beck could hardly keep up with the orders.

One day Mrs Whisker went to look for some food near her home which was a mixture of wood and leaves and it was close to a little river. Inside the river were many fish. Sonny-pink liked to swim and fish at the same time. When she got to the river she immediately jumped into the river and started to swim. The water was very nice and clean and very warm. Suddenly Sonny-pink stopped swimming for in front of her was something shining brightly in the water. She swam quickly towards the object to try and find out what it was. It was a pure pink-gold diamond necklace. Mrs Whisker had no idea what she was looking at, but she picked it up and put it on her neck, jumped out of the water and ran home as fast as she could to show the item to her kittens. The kittens were delighted with the necklace and from that day Sonny-pink wore the necklace.

Magic Island has no nation, so many rich powerful nations were interested to claim it as their own. Many businessmen visited the island to consider if it was suitable for a tourist industry.

Mrs Whisker, Baby Puss I and Baby Puss II had often seen many people visiting the island. The cats always stayed away from the visitors, in fact they hid in the long grass watching what was going on. Each time they were very worried especially Sonny-pink. She was frightened that her kittens would be taken away from her.

One sunny afternoon Mrs Whisker, Baby Puss I and Baby Puss II were enjoying the hot sun when all of a sudden they heard human voices. They tried to hide but it was too late. A huge man ran up to them shouting in a nasty voice, "Come here, cats." The cats did not understand human language but of course understood danger. They were horrified. Out of the blue a magnificent voice said in cat language, "The necklace around your neck, give to him." The voice seemed to be coming from the Grass Hopper Forest. Sonny-pink quickly did as the voice demanded. She removed the necklace and dropped it on the ground, picked up her kittens and ran as fast as she could into Grass Hopper Forest. The cats could hear laughing from the man. Sonny-pink, Baby Puss I and Baby Puss II were so shocked at what they had experienced, they were unable to speak, they just sat down and cried.

The voice that Mrs Whisker had heard was the voice of the good forest fairy. Fairies are always willing to help people and animals in great danger. Also fairies can speak human and animal languages.

The story goes about the gold and diamond necklace known as the Rose Petal Necklace, due to its pink-gold colour, that it belonged to Queen Victoria, Queen of England. The queen had an argument with one of her jewellers. He stole the necklace, left Britain by boat in a hurry and unfortunately drowned at sea. The necklace was lost at sea. After several years the Rose Petal Necklace landed in the little river near Sonny-pink's home.

The Rose Petal Necklace represents good and bad fortune.

True:

A grasshopper is a jumping chirping insect.

Magic Island is a fairyland island.

A fairy is a small supernatural being with magical powers.

A necklace, an ornament worn around the neck.

The Miracle of the Carnation Flowers

"Hello," said the excited voice on the telephone. "This is Mr Kidyou speaking from Zoo Island, am I speaking to Mrs Pole Jellyrose of Melbourne?"

"Yes speaking," replied Pole.

On Zoo Island in the Pacific Ocean, a perfume company had advertised locally and overseas about their invention – a perfume tonic named Paradise Glow Perfume Tonic. The tonic was especially made for flowers to improve their natural perfume. The treatment was for one year, 24 bottles, the cost US$4,800 and US$150 for postage and handling. The guarantee was for 24 hours!

Mrs Jellyrose, like thousands of other trusting people, believed in the advertisement and immediately purchased the product.

Mrs Jellyrose had received the product the previous day and needed more details on how to use the tonic. Pole said to Mr Kidyou, "Yesterday I left a message with your secretary. I asked how many drops of perfume per day are required for my carnations?"

Mr Kidyou replied, "Two drops of tonic in a bucket of warm soapy water, mix, then spray the carnations."

For several weeks Pole sprayed her carnations. Now some months had passed and the pretty pale pink carnations had started to change their colour to an awful orange-green colour plus the flowers had a terrible smell of fish.

Pole had spent a large sum of money all for nothing. She was angry and in desperation she again contacted the company. A secretary answered the telephone saying the Manager, Mr

Telltales, was in a meeting and could not be disturbed and that Mrs Jellyrose would be contacted the following day. In fact Mr Telltales was hiding somewhere in Europe for he knew that his so-called miracle tonic was a fake and he was living very well in a five-star hotel off honest people's money. He also had a problem – his holiday visa was due to expire the following day.

That night Pole had an idea. She decided to spray the carnations with Tasmanian milk and her own secret tea recipe.

Mrs Jellyrose was from Tasmania, the Australian island state. Her parents had been farmers, they had a dairy farm and the milk was delicious and creamy, and as all milk has calcium that is good for humans, why not flowers also?

For over two weeks Pole sprayed her carnations with Tasmanian milk and her own secret recipe but still no improvements!

The following day Mrs Jellyrose happened to be looking out of her kitchen window, when to her amazement she saw that the odd-coloured weak-looking carnations had grown overnight into magnificent 30 foot high flowers! News about the miracle of the carnation flowers spread all over Australia and overseas. People from everywhere came to look at Mrs Jellyrose's carnation flowers.

True:

Tasmania is an Australian island state.

Fairy tale name: Zoo Island.

Trip to the Sun via New Zealand

"I have an announcement to make," said Mr Te Rat, a Maori rat. Te told his friends he had decided to visit the Sun!

"The Sun!" said his friends in amazement. "You must be mistaken, the sun is boiling hot, you would not last one minute near it, no one has ever visited the Sun."

Te was determined to try his home-made rocket which had taken him six years to build in his backyard.

The day arrived for Te to go to the Sun, the whole neighbourhood had come to his home to wish him well and see him off on a journey of a lifetime.

Te had a huge suitcase full of clothes and food. Most of his clothes were woollen just in case he caught fire! Wool does not catch fire, often a small fire can be put out by placing a woollen blanket or woollen garment on the fire.

Te was all dressed up and ready to go! He also brought with him his camera, as he planned to take hundreds of photographs of the Sun.

Te's best friend Te Papa lit the rocket, Te got inside the rocket, and it shot into the air leaving Te behind! The journey took ten hours for the rocket to reach the Sun.

News spread all over New Zealand and the world that Mr Te Rat of Christchurch, South Island had invented a homemade rocket that had gone to the Sun!

NASA in America was contacted by Christchurch Radio. NASA launches rockets into space, so they were able to televise Te's rocket going to the Sun and coming back to Earth.

The Mayor of Christchurch gave Te a medal for his hard work.

True:

Christchurch, New Zealand is the south island.

A Maori is the native of New Zealand.

NASA is in America, it launches rockets into space.

John the Gorilla: His True Story

Once upon a time in West Africa lived a miniature cross-eyed gorilla named John. He lived with his parents, fifteen sisters and nine brothers. They lived in a huge forest surrounded by coconut trees, banana trees and other tropical fruit trees and a very large river. The gorilla family would often go to the river to swim, only John was unable to swim.

John had two disabilities. He was born very tiny and had double vision. Having such disabilities did not prevent him from having the ambition to become a swimmer even though he was terrified of water! The first thing he wanted to do was get rid of his fear of water.

One day John came across a small stream. It was partly covered by a huge tree that had fallen down due to the recent annual cyclone. John stood on the tree and dived into the water. As soon as he hit the water he felt terrible panic run through his body but he was determined to remain in the water for the water was very clean and warm and nearby birds could be heard singing and the hot sun shone through the trees. In fact it was a perfect day to learn to swim.

John was so enjoying the atmosphere that he fell asleep! In the dream he was a champion swimmer enjoying the attention of being presented with a bunch of bananas by his best friend Tolipi. All of a sudden John woke up. To his horror, he found himself in the middle of the sea, John was miles away from dry land. Terrified he swam to shore!

John overcame his fear of water and became a very good swimmer.

True:

West Africa is part of the African continent.

Cross-eyed, double vision.

Atmosphere, environment.

Cyclone, a violent storm.

Miniature, tiny.

Stream, water running into a river or the sea.

Disabilities, things that incapacitate.

Dame the Giant Ghost Fly

Once upon a time a huge ghost fly named Dame stayed in a small old-fashioned wooden house in Queensland. Dame's place was in the attic, a room full of old leather suitcases, old newspapers, photographs of war heroes, books and maps.

The old wooden house had belonged to Colonel James Roberts, a gentleman of good character and great wealth. He was a single man who gave away most of his wealth to charities as well as raising funds for charities by playing his piano. The Colonel was also a trained music teacher and people came from miles to listen to his magnificent piano music.

Colonel James Roberts had a very long life, but suddenly at the age of ninety-seven and a half years old he went to heaven. A week later Dame also passed away. in insect age he was 101 years old, but Dame's ghost remained in the attic. The Colonel had adopted Dame and had turned the attic into a bedroom for Dame.

Dame was an unusual fly. He had a very high I.Q. which was 175 in human terms, and due to his quick understanding Colonel Roberts was able to teach the giant fly how to read and write, especially how to read maps. Like all army officers they love maps and wanted to share the joy of map-reading with everyone including a genius fly. Within a few weeks Dame could read maps like a professional army officer. The Colonel and Dame the giant fly had great conversations on how to save the world.

When Dame passed away his ghost would spend its days in the attic and continue reading all sorts of maps. Sometimes the Colonel's ghost would join Dame's ghost and they would continue reading maps and having great conversations on how to save the world.

When Dame's ghost wanted a break from the attic he would fly around Queensland enjoying the magnificent scenery, then return very late at night to the attic.

This is Dame's story when he was alive.

Dame lived near a Queensland forest named Goodwill Forest and had a disability where he could only fly upside down. He longed to fly upright like other flies.

Several months had passed and Dame decided to go to Goodwill Forest and search for food. When he arrived at the forest he could see in the distance a huge tree that had been cut down. Surrounding the tree were small pieces of wood. Dame had an idea – he would make himself a wooden bed. He flew up to the tree and after a few minutes searching for the right size wood he found it. He also required a soft piece of twig so that he could tie the piece of wood on his back and take the wood back to his home.

As he tied the wood to his back something amazing happened – the weight of the wood turned Dame upright! Dame was overjoyed. For the first time in his life he would be able to fly upright like a normal fly. He changed his idea of making a wooden bed and instead made himself a magnificent pair of wings. Dame flew across the world to try out his new wings, and became a world famous film star. People just loved Dame for his courage and determination and that is why Colonel Roberts adopted him.

Today in the Queensland Museum Dame's photograph can be seen in the insect section, and now let us remember him as the greatest fly that ever lived.

The Village Ghost

Good afternoon, I am Henrietta Marie de la Vigne, a well known Mauritian clairvoyant working with the present Mauritian Prime Minister helping him to make better decisions that will enrich the island's tourist industry etc.

One afternoon while in my study, the ghost of my late cousin Veronique de Vacoas came to visit me. Often, her ghost came to visit me, and she would spend many happy hours discussing many important topics including our family tree past and present. This is Veronique's story:

Australia 1985

It was a fine summer's day and Miss Veronique de Vacoas was celebrating her 120th birthday. She lived in a very nice Melbourne nursing home named View of Paradise. The nursing home had belonged to Count Richard Bones-Smyth and his two resident employees, Mr and Mrs Allah Dunie.

The Dunies had immigrated from Saudi Arabia to Australia in the 1970s and every two-to-three years they went on holiday to Jeddah, Saudi Arabia. They had kept their Jeddah house and when they were older they would retire to Jeddah.

Mr Allah Dunie was about 56 years old; he was a very pleasant fellow, and was somewhat short with a huge moustache. Allah was a qualified landscape gardener, the view of Paradise Gardens was truly beautiful with water fountains, fruit trees and bright red roses. The view of Paradise Gardens had won 'Best Garden in the Neighbourhood' competition for the past six years.

Mrs Reza Dunie was about 54 years old, she was a huge jolly woman. Reza was the Head Housekeeper. She loved to bake cakes, especially birthday cakes. Reza made her own designs, they were magnificent

Australia 1955

In 1955 Veronique de Vacoas emigrated from Mauritius to Australia. She was a trained primary school teacher; she loved her career and decided to remain single. Many men found her intelligent and attractive, but long ago she had wanted to marry her cousin Charles Castleraye.

Mauritius from 1885 to early 1955.

Until 1885 Veronique's family name had been de Maison. The family name change occurred because her parents Pilo and Lordes had inherited a tiny village where they lived named Vacoas. Pilo's late father had been a billionaire named Mr Roach de Maison and due to his wealth he was able to purchase Vacoas.

Mr de Maison had also been a scientist and an inventor of three pegs:

Peg No. 1 named heavy duty clothes peg.
Peg No. 2 named delicate duty clothes peg.

Both pegs were made from soft wood but strong enough not to break. The cushion was in the inner side of the pegs made of soft cotton material to protect it from falling apart.

And finally:

Peg No. 3 named threefold peg stand – the blanket and the sheet peg. A miniature wooden frame with rounded hollow handles for a person to place their fingers inside the hollow handles to adjust the spring inside the peg frame if required.

Mr de Maison had been a very pleasant man, he and Lordes had given away large amounts of cash to charities and often the couple would hold birthday parties at their beautiful home for the less fortunate.

Pilo and Lordes had only one child, Veronique Pilo Isabelle. The couple never discussed their wealth in front of 'Veri', a nickname they gave her, the couple wanted Veronique to study hard and have a career and not expect them to give her funds to do as she pleased and always help people in need.

The village of Vacoas

Vacoas was well established with good roads and the villagers were a happy people, until one day one of the villagers, Veronique's cousin Charles Castleraye, decided to go to Egypt. He was never seen nor heard from again. Due to this terrible tragedy an awful sadness overshadowed the tiny village and Veronique never got over the loss of her cousin Charles Rene Phillip Andrew Castleraye.

1925 Mauritius and Egypt

In 1925 Charles Castleraye left Mauritius for Egypt... five years had passed and one day the de Vacoas family received a telephone call from Cairo, the capital of Egypt. The Cairo Hotel Manager informed them that a tourist had visited a pyramid and came across a little wooden box. Inside the box was a letter addressed to Miss Veronique de Vacoas, Vacoas Mauritius signed Charles Castleraye, Egypt 1925. The family was overjoyed with the news.

A few weeks passed and the box and the letter were delivered to the de Vacoas residence. Immediately Lordes placed the box in her fish pond for good luck, in some quarters it is believed that placing an item in a garden pond that belongs to a missing person will bring back the missing person.

Sixty years had passed and so it seemed that the good luck to find Charles had finally run out.

Australia 1985 (continued)

It was now 1985 and it was over 60 years since the disappearance of Charles; if he had been alive he would have been 140 years old, which of course would have been impossible to even consider. Veronique had hoped to marry him and now she was in a nursing home celebrating her 120th birthday.

"Wake up, Miss de Vacoas," said Reza Dunie. "Happy Birthday." Mrs Dunie had made a huge pink and white birthday cake in a shape of a bow with silver and gold coloured marzipan flowers on top of the cake, truly a masterpiece.

A few hours later Count Bones-Smyth came to visit Veronique. He carried a wooden box like the one in Mr and Mrs Pilo de Vacoas's fish pond back in Vacoas. The Count opened the box and removed a very pretty necklace, an Egyptian necklace. Miss de Vacoas was very shocked, it was only then that she recognised the man standing in front of her. The Count sat down and told her a very strange sad tale.

Miss de Vacoas had only been in the nursing home for eight weeks, she had been living in her own home until she had fallen down and broken her left arm. She then decided that it was time for her to live in a nursing home, she kept her home and rented it to students.

The moment Miss de Vacoas arrived at View of Paradise, the Count had recognised her, but he had taken his time to reveal the truth. He was really Charles Castleraye. In 1925 he had gone to Egypt to visit the pyramids but he had done something dishonest. He had stolen some of the treasure found in the pyramids that belonged to the ancient noble and royal families of

Egypt. He had sold the treasure and become very rich but due to this greed he had an Egyptian curse placed on him. The curse was written in an ancient Egyptian dialect on one of the pyramid walls. When translated into modern English language the message read "Whoever enters this chamber and removes any of the treasure will remain on earth forever." Charles had laughed at the curse, he made a fortune and changed his name to Richard Bones-Smyth after a British 1795 navigator Sir Lucian Rio Bones-Smyth.

Charles came to Melbourne to make a new life for himself, but with his dishonest wealth it became a burden. He became very distressed. He and Mr and Mrs Dunie purchased View of Paradise Nursing Home. Charles owned 80% of the home, the Dunies owned 20% of the nursing home. Also Charles had given away the rest of the funds from the sale of the stolen treasure, for he had had enough of wealth. He wished that he had never been dishonest, nor could he get rid of the Egyptian curse placed on him. He was now 140 years old and would remain on earth forever.

The following day Veronique left the nursing home never to return. The day she left View of Paradise she contacted the police to have Charles arrested and sent to prison. He had been on the run for over 60 years.

Two things that are to be noted: Miss de Vacoas had been given a very long life by God. He had guided her to the nursing home to have Charles arrested and placed in prison, and lastly View of Paradise Nursing Home was shut down and sold to larger nursing home organisation; 80% of the funds that belonged to Charles were distributed to charities because prisoners cannot have any funds from the sale of their property/ies, especially stolen funds! The 20% of the funds that belonged to the Dunies were given to them for they were innocent. They had no idea about Charles's past. Shortly after the sale of View of Paradise, Allah and Reza returned to Jeddah, Saudi Arabia.

People often say that God works in mysterious ways and certainly that is true.

True:

Mauritius is in the Indian Ocean.

Vacoas is a tiny village in Mauritius.

Marzipan: sweet substance made of pounded almonds.

The 'village' a-host.